RUPTURED SOULS

Ruptured souls bestow nothing upon you,
they plea for your help.

By: Mohannad Al Azab

Translation to English: Adam Lebzo

Order this book online at www.trafford.com
or email orders@trafford.com

Most Trafford titles are also available at major online book retailers.

Printed in the United States of America.

ISBN: 978-1-4907-1740-1 (sc)
ISBN: 978-1-4907-1741-8 (hc)
ISBN: 978-1-4907-1742-5 (e)

Library of Congress Control Number: 2013918948

Trafford rev. 12/27/2013

 www.trafford.com

North America & international
toll-free: 1 888 232 4444 (USA & Canada)
fax: 812 355 4082

Dedication

Ruptured souls bestow nothing upon you, they plea for your help.

الأرواح المشروخة، لا تهديكم شيئا...ولكنها تستغيث

Introduction

"Do not be afraid if you're wounded. Otherwise, how will light sneak onto your heart?"

-- Jalaluldeen Al Roomi

"لا تجزع من جرحك، وإلا فكيف للنور أن يتسلل إلى باطنك"

جلال الدين الرومي

My message

رسالتي

Pondering existence, **seeking** wisdom, and **sharing** all this knowledge with the world.

تأمل الوجود، والبحث عن الحكمة ومشاركة الناس هذه التجربة

Author's Biography:

نبذة عن الكاتب

Mohannad Al Azab, Jordanian writer, born in 1970, specialized in writing epigrams and very short stories. He began his writing carrier since the earliest days of his life as he persevered to ponder the universe and life with all its details and meanings.

Mohannad Al Azab had his first book published "the night of the full wolf" in 2006, which won him **Naji Numan Prize Of Modern Literature** in Lebanon. Afterwards, his second book "The visions of the bat" was published followed by "Solo" in 2013 which is a collection of very short stories.

The controversial writings of Mohannad Al Azab have caused a huge jumble in the Arab cultural society and were studied and reviewed by many famous critics. The writings of Mohannad Al Azab are short yet dense emotionally and spiritually. It snatches the reader unto foreign dimensions and opens a door of meditative experiences.

"Ruptured souls" is another add to Mohannad's series wherein he casts around for wisdom in everything he mulls over like creatures, event, and daily life details.

مهند العزب كاتب أردني من مواليد مدينة السلط (1970)، متخصص في كتابة الشذرات والقصص القصيرة جدا. بدأ مسيرته في الكتابة منذ نعومة اظافره، حيث دأب في تأمل الكون والحياة بكل تفاصيلها من حوله ، حيث كان يمارس لعبة الغميضة مع المعاني التي تتمثل في الكائنات، ويلاحق الأفكار أينما وجدها، خلف شجرة أو تحت حجر بجانب النهر، أو في ذاته المتوارية. نشر مهند العزب كتابه الأول"ليلة اكتمال الذئب" في 2006 ، الكتاب الذي حصل على جائزة ناجي نعمان للأدب الجديد في لبنان. وفي 2010 نشر كتابه الثاني"رؤى الخفاش"، وفي 2013 نشر "صولو" وهو مجموعة قصص قصيرة جدا. وقد أثارت كتابات مهند العزب جدلا واسعا في الوسط الثقافي العربي، حيث تناولها عدد من النقاد المعروفين، وقد لفتت انتباههم وإعجابهم، إذا تتميز كتابات العزب بالاختزال والكثافة المعنوية والشعورية، فهي تخطف القارئ إلى عوالم لا مألوفة، و تفتح أمامه بابا من التجارب التأملية التي تدفع الإنسان لاكتشاف ذاته، وتجعله أكثر شجاعة في رؤيتها دون مكياج. والأكثر من ذلك، أنها تحرّض القارئ على الانحياز للحرية كقيمة أساسية، وللإنسان الحقيقي الذي يمثل تجسيدا لهذه القيمة. ويأتي كتابه هذا"أرواح مشروخة" في سياق كتاباته السابقة نفسه، بحيث يبحث فيه عن الحكمة في كل ما يتأمله من كائنات وأحداث وكل ما يمر عليه من تجارب وتفاصيل حياتية، ويواصل مهند العزب بحثه عن أسرار الكون وعن الحكمة المحجوبة من خلال كتاباته المميزة

Translator's Biography

نبذة عن المترجم

Adam Nart Lebzo, a 21 years old writer, poet, playwright, martial artist, translator, and researcher. The Founder of "Ragnarok Translation and Literary Agency" located in Amman, Jordan.

Adam Lebzo has founded Ragnarok Agency in 2013 on a mission to spread the writings and creativity of Jordanian writers to the whole world by breaking the main gab, Language.

"Ruptured Souls" is Ragnarok's debut and pride. Hopefully it will show the whole world that Jordan is full of underground creativeness and surprises.

آدم نارت لبزو، ولد عام 1992، هو كاتب وشاعر ومترجم. وهو أيضا مؤسس "راجناروك للترجمة والوكالة الأدبية" في عمان، الأردن

لقد عمل آدم لبزو جاهدا لإنشاء راجناروك عام 2013 حتى تكون منارة تُظهر للعالم أجمع الإبداعات الكتابية المدفونة في الأردن عن طريق كسر الحاجز الأساسي، ألا وهو اللغة.

"أرواح مشروخة" هو الكتاب الاول لوكالة راجناروك وهو فخرها كذلك. على أمل أن يثبت هذا الكتاب للعالم أجمع أن الأردن بلد معطاء ومليء بالإبداع والجمال والعقل والحكمة.

1. The traveler who failed to arrive, it's enough that he's shown the road.

    - السائر الذي لم يصل يكفي أنه قد أشار إلى الدرب

2. The discomfited reads the memoirs of the victors with mixed feelings.

    - الخاسرون يقرؤون مذكرات المنتصر بمشاعر متناقضة

3. I do not know why my conscience likes to awake when I want to sleep.

    - لا أعلم لماذا ضميري لا يحلو له الاستيقاظ الا عندما افكر أن أنام

4. Every time the runner launches, he doubts the direction.

    - كلما انطلق العداء شك بالاتجاه

5. Even if I walked on water, I would fear digression.

    - حتى إن مشيت على الماء أخشى أن أتوه

6. Perhaps it's wise to believe of the fatuity of many things.

   ● ربما جزء من الحكمة أن نؤمن بسخافة كثير من الاشياء

7. Even the last runner outran all the hesitators whom didn't join the race.

   ● حتى العداء الأخير سبق كل المترددين في خوض السباق

8. Even a bird with a broken wing would eschew standing on a broken branch.

   ● حتى العصفور مكسور الجناح يتجنب الوقوف على الغصن المكسور

9. At the end, everything is topped with dust.

   ● في النهاية كل شيء يعلوه الغبار

10. A life boat wishes the ship would sink but within its heart, it fears drowning.

    ● يود قارب النجاة لو تغرق السفينة لكنه في قرارة نفسه يخاف الغرق

2

11. How wretched the lifeboat is? Watches the sea but cannot touch it.

- كم هو تعيس قارب النجاة, يرى البحر ولا يلمسه

12. No creature is better than a turtle for a long-distance race.

- لا مخلوق أصلح من السلحفاة لسباق المسافات الطويلة

13. Maybe because a turtle knows that the road will never end, it walks at leisure.

- ربما لأن السلحفاة تدرك أن لا نهاية للمسير, تمشي على مهل

14. An empty vase on a balcony looks down with keen interest at a rose that is about to bloom.

- تنظر المزهرية الفارغة من على الشرفة باهتمام بالغ للوردة التي أوشكت على التفتح

15. Before his death, he took a deep breath.

- قبيل وفاته أخذ نفسا عميقا

3

16. Before the shut door, an open horizon.

أمام الباب المغلق أفق مفتوح

17. The mute leads a silent protest and shouts aloud.

الأبكم يقود مظاهرة صامتة ويصرخ فيها

18. A broken verdant branch.

غصن مكسور مورق

19. Committing suicide only works at the last time.

الإقدام على الانتحار لا ينجح إلا في المرة الأخيرة

20. A good watch-smith, yet always late.

يتقن إصلاح الساعات ولكنه دوما متأخر

21. Always stand still and your limp won't show.

قف مكانك دوما ولن يظهر العرج الذي بقدمك •

22. I don't think my *creative* friend has bought books as much as he has bought cigarettes. However, he suffers from creativity and does not suffer from Lung cancer.

لا أعتقد أن صديقي "المبدع" اشترى كتباً بربع ما اشترى من السجائر, ومع • ذلك يعاني من الإبداع ولا يعاني من سرطان الرئة

23. Even the last runner has the right to finish the race.

حتى المتسابق الأخير من حقه إنهاء السباق •

24. Even some fish try, from time to time, to get out of water.

حتى بعض السمك يحاول من حين الى آخر الخروج من الماء •

25. Even a loudspeaker needs you to speak.

حتى مكبر الصوت يحتاج منك أن تتكلم •

26. Some huntsmen are more scared than the prey itself.

● بعض الصيادين أكثر هلعا من الفريسة

27. The house is pulled down, the people are gone, and the dog is still barking at pedestrians.

● تهدم المنزل ورحل السكان وما زال الكلب ينبح على المارة.

28. How brave chess players are, they never surrender no matter how much blood is shed!

● ما أشجع لاعبي الشطرنج لا ينسحبون مهما سال من الدماء.

29. Someone got bit by a snake so you may have a soft belt.

● هناك من لدغه الثعبان لتحصل أنت على حزام ناعم.

30. Even a shipwreck is good material for a boat.

● حتى حطام السفينة يصلح لصنع قارب

31. Even a dried river can lead you to the sea.

- حتى النهر الذي جف يمكنه أن يدلك على البحر

32. Do you know what makes a comedian play even funnier? A sad scene.

- يزيد المسرحية الكوميدية فكاهة مشهد حزين

33. Even when a bird falls, he still has a pair of wings.

- حتى عندما يسقط الطائر يظل له جناحان

34. Everytime I buy a book about losing weight, I pile weight and books.

- كلما اشتريت كتابا حول كيفية فقد بعض الوزن, أراني أراكم الوزن والكتب

35. Life is not our foe. So if life beat us, we've been into a wrong fight.

- الحياة ليست خصمنا, لذا إذا هزمتنا الحياة نكون قد خضنا معركة خاطئة

36.   Sometimes we arrive when we stop running.

●   أحيانا نصل حينما نكف عن الجري

37.   The ship that sailed afar maybe has struggled to leave the
dock.

●   السفينة التي أبحرت بعيداً قد تكون عانت في الخروج من الميناء

38.   Even masks are like us, rarely does a grumpy man pick a
smiling mask.

●   حتى الأقنعة تشبهنا, نادرا ما يختار الرجل العابس قناعا مبتسما

39.   We are trees... Our childhood is our roots.

●   نحن شجر, طفولتنا جذورنا.

40.   Some humans are like stars, they might look close, but in
fact they are far apart.

●   بعض البشر كالنجوم, قد تبدو متقاربة ولكن قد يكون بينها مسافات شاسعة.

41. I do not know if there's mayhem in the universe, but I've a headache.

- لا أعرف إذا كان هناك صخب في الكون ولكن لدي صداع

42. He unveiled a continent, his tomb is still unknown.

- اكتشف قارة وقبره ما زال مجهولاً

43. There's a snail – that appears to be hasty compared to his peers.

- هناك حلزون – يبدو بالنسبة لبقية صحبه مستعجلاً!

44. The best shoes do not guarantee you won't get lost.

- أفضل الأحذية لا تضمن لك ألا تضيع

45. Don't ponder mortal things.

- لا تمعن النظر بالزائل

46. All these scars, not because I didn't stand, but because I didn't withdraw.

- كل تلك الندوب ليس لأني لم أصمد بل لأني لم أنسحب

47. Usually I imagine the woman who didn't have children, a great mother.

- عادة أتخيل المرأة التي لم تنجب أما عظيمة

48. Amid traffic a semi-crippled man marches between cars with his crutch.

- في زحمة السير يتقدم رجل شبه مقعد بين السيارات بعكازته

49. The obstacle is not in our feet, thereby it can be overcame.

- العثرة ليست بأقدامنا لذا يمكن تخطيها

50. Even when the ship sails, it takes the anchor along.

- حتى والسفينة تبحر تأخذ المرساة معها

51.   Do glasses really improve our vision of this world?

●   هل تحسن فعلا النظارات رؤيتنا للعالم؟

52.   Some humans are like some ships, never arrive, never sail.

●   بعض البشر مثل بعض السفن. لا تصل ولا تبحر

53.   Even a broken vase panics roses.

●   حتى المزهرية المكسورة تثير ذعر الورد

54.   A runner asks himself: How much should I run to win the 100m race?

●   يسأل العداء نفسه كم يجب أن أجري لأفوز في سباق المائة متر؟

55.   Because it lives long we think it doesn't age... The turtle.

●   لأنها تعمر طويلا نظنها لا تشيخ. هي السلحفاة

56. In the vase, roses do not wither, they suicide!

في المزهرية لا تذبل الورود ولكن تنتحر

57. Because my house has no garden... I wither.

لأن بيتي بلا حديقة ... أذبل!

58. She, who deserves a rose, deserves much.

التي تستحق الوردة تستحق الكثير

59. I might be thirsty, but the fount is not my borne.

قد أكون عطشاً, لكن وجهتي ليست النبع

60. It doesn't shame a boat to swing.

لا يعيب القارب ان يتأرجح

61. Those who fear sailing can make boats.

حتى الذين يخافون الإبحار يمكن أن يصنعوا المراكب •

62. Even fish need skill for not to drown.

حتى السمك يحتاج للمهارة كي لا يغرق •

63. Do not cling overmuch unto things, a deserted nest has done its job.

لا تتشبث بالأشياء أكثر مما يجب ٫ فالعش المهجور أدى واجبه •

64. A broken branch does not stop the tree from blossoming.

الغصن المكسور لا يمنع الشجرة أن تزهر •

65. My bullying made me bleed.

تنمري جعلني أنزف •

66. Don't look at the one ahead of you, maybe his path is longer.

- لا تنظر لمن يتقدمك, ربما دربه أطول

67. The stairs amaze me, they divided the problem of raising simply.

- يدهشني الدرج. قسم مشكلة الصعود بكل بساطة.

68. Learn from the turtle not to attract much attention when you go on.

- تعلم من السلحفاة ألا تثير انتباه الكثيرين حين تتقدم

69. Even fire teaches us not to let anybody get too close.

- حتى النار تعلمنا ألا تدع أحدا يقترب منك أكثر من اللازم

70. When you know exactly what's your message, you'll quit being the mailman.

- حين تعرف بالضبط ما هي رسالتك, ستكف عن ان تكون ساعي البريد.

71. What does it matter for the fish in its small tank, if it's on a plane that crosses continents.

● ماذا يهم السمكة في دورقها الضيق, إذا كانت على متن طائرة تقطع القارات.

72. A magician cannot believe what he adeptly did.

● ساحر لا يصدق ما اتقن فعله

73. Everybody tricked him but the magician.

● خدعه كل من عرفه إلا الساحر

74. A magician does not believe in truth.

● الساحر لا يصدق الحقيقة

75. What makes a drowned ship even more sorrowful is the fact that it didn't get far from the dock.

● مما يزيد من حزن السفينة الغارقة, أنها لم تبتعد عن الميناء

76. I don't believe I am lost and someone is tracking me.

- لا أصدق أنا ضائع وهناك من يتعقبني

77. Our wounds sometimes lead us to overrate our ability of curing people.

- تدفعنا أحيانا جراحنا للمبالغة بالادعاء بقدرتنا على شفاء الآخرين

78. Only defeat teaches us revision, no revision in victory.

- الخسارة وحدها تعلمنا المراجعة, لا مراجعة في الانتصار

79. Dreamt of emigration, now suffers from it.

- يحلم بالغربة ويعانيها الآن

80. He has an artificial heart, and doesn't know if he is cold-hearted or not.

- يحمل قلبا صناعيا ولا يعرف أنه كان قاسي القلب

81. The loner is hunting down homing pigeons; hoping to find a
    letter!

· الوحيد يصطاد الحمام الزاجل عله يجد أية رسالة

82. He has an orotund voice, but he's always silent.

· صوته جهوري لكنه دوما صامت

83. Before the microphone, the mute stands in awful silence.

· أمام المايكروفون يقف الأبكم بصمت عظيم

84. Does the silent always tell the truth?

· هل الصامت دوما يقول الحق؟

85. Digression in shortcuts.

· تيه في الدروب المختصرة

86. Even in the eyes of the oppressed I glance cruelty sometimes.

- حتى في عيون المظلوم أحيانا ألمح قسوة

87. A stander looking ahead, and a walker looking around.

- واقف ينظر امامه وسائر يتلفت

88. When a bee stings you, *without a reason*, remember all the honey you gorged on all your life.

- حين تلسعك النحلة – بلا سبب – تذكر كل العسل الذي أكلته في عمرك

89. A turtle with a limp.

- سلحفاة وبها عرج.

90. The fish that escaped the net will always be the most terrified.

- السمكة التي هربت من الشباك ستظل دوما الأكثر ذعرا

91.   On the ship of life nothing is guaranteed, not even life boats.

● على سفينة الحياة لا شيء مضمون حتى قوارب النجاة

92.   Get away from the snake, because every year it changes its skin, not its thoughts.

● ابتعد عن الأفعى لأنها كل سنة تغير جلدها لا أفكارها

93.   Maybe it wasn't the best tree, but maybe it will be the best boat.

● ربما لم تكن أفضل الاشجار ولكن ربما تكون افضل القوارب

94.   Even when you limp, and after exerting reasonable effort, you'll be stunned with the distance you've crossed.

● حتى وأنت تعرج وبعد بذل جهد معقول ستتعجب من المسافة التي ستقطعها

95.   The boat that anchored by the deck might drown as well.

● القارب الذي يرسو في الميناء قد يغرق أيضا

96. Even old lanterns are good enough to light new paths.

حتى القناديل القديمة تصلح لإنارة درب جديد

97. In darkness, everything is there. You just have to ponder.

في العتمة كل شيء موجود ما عليك إلا أن تتأمل

98. I think therefore I am... an outcast!

أنا افكر... اذا أنا منبوذ

99. The one that climbed the mountain and reached the top isn't braver than the one who fell at the first abyss.

الذي صعد الجبل ووصل للقمة ليس أكثر شجاعة من الذي سقط عند أول هاوية

100. Wishes are much heavier than defeats.

إن الأماني أكثر ثقلا من الهزائم

101.   The turtle is not slow, but *your* time is limited.

السلحفاة ليست بطيئة لكن أنت وقتك محدود ●

102.   Since there are no major battles in the life of the modern
       man, he is defeated by the details of his day.

لأنه لا معارك كبرى في حياة الانسان المعاصر تهزمه تفاصيل يومه ●

103.   The butterfly pities the fire that is about to die out.

تشفق الفراشة على النار التي أوشكت على الانطفاء ●

104.   The most ferocious wolf leaves the deer after it saw it
       closely.

أشرس الذئاب هو الذي يترك الغزالة بعد أن رأته عن كثب ●

105.   You must build the bridge in your imagination before you
       reach the abyss.

يجب أن تبني الجسر في خيالك قبل أن تصل الهاوية ●

21

106. No one should stay outside in this freezing cold, not even the snowman.

   • يجب ألا يبقى أحد خارج المنزل في هذا البرد حتى رجل الثلج

107. On the threshold, the Snowman stands and gazes at warmth until it melts.

   • على العتبة يقف رجل الثلج وينظر إلى الدفء حتى يذوب

108. No matter how much we're quenched, we are afraid to leave the fount.

   • مهما ارتوينا نخاف أن نسافر بعيدا عن النبع

109. The Snowman's problem is not the cold, its loneliness.

   • مشكلة رجل الثلج ليس أنه يقف في البرد بل أنه وحيد

110. What do you know! Maybe the bird is amid the sky because he cannot find a branch to alight on.

   • ما أدراك ربما الطائر ظلّ يحلق في كبد السماء لأنه لم يجد غصنا يقف عليه

111.   Poor is the waterfall! Much are satisfied with his speed, but
       he is not satisfied with his direction.

- يالخسارة الشلال, الكثيرون راضون عن سرعته ولكنه غير راض عن
  اتجاهه

112.   Since we are lone, we twaddle much.

- لأننا وحيدون نثرثر أكثر

113.   Quenched Flames!

- نار مطفأة

114.   Fire does not want to live long, it wants to deflagrate.

- لا تريد النار أن تعيش طويلا تريد أن تتأجج

115.   The burnt will cry when fire deflagrates, and will sob when
       it dies.

- سيبكي المحترق حينما تتأجج النار وينتحب حينما تنطفىء

116. The burnt prefers meat medium-rare.

● المحترق يفضل اللحم قبل أن ينضج بقليل

117. He does not add salt to raw meat... The burnt.

● لا يضيف الملح على اللحم غير الناضج, هو المحترق

118. Only real flowers wilt.

● الأزهار الحقيقية هي فقط التي تذبل

119. The rose knows well that it will wilt, thus it blossoms sorely.

● تدرك الوردة أنها ستذبل لذا تتفتح بألم

120. A cactus asks a rose: Which is harder, Wilt or thirst?

● تسأل الصبارة الوردة أيهما أصعب العطش أم الذبول؟

121. Sad as a broken branch on the onset of spring, blooms a little, suffers a lot.

   • حزين مثل غصن مكسور في بداية الربيع, يزهر قليلا ويتألم أكثر

122. The eve is frigid, maybe because I am sad.

   • الليلة باردة... ربما لأنني حزين

123. I didn't find a door, and everybody is giving me keys.

   • لم أجد باباً والكل يعطيني المفاتيح

124. Even a punctured ship tempts me to sail.

   • حتى السفينة المثقوبة تغريني بالإبحار

125. The sweetest fount is at the depth of the ocean.

   • النبع الأعذب... في قعر المحيط

126. A tracker lost in the city.

- قصاص الأثر تائه في المدينة

127. A pawn travels far on the chess board, not to face the enemy, but to reach the edge and jump away.

- يذهب الجندي بعيدا على رقعة الشطرنج ليس ليواجه الأعداء ولكن ليصل للحافة ويقفز مبتعدا

128. The general went frantic when he realized that a pawn is missing from the chess board.

- يجن جنون القائد العسكري حين يجد أن جندياً مفقود من على رقعة الشطرنج

129. I do not eat honey, yet a bee stung me.

- لا آكل العسل ومع ذلك لسعتني نحلة

130. On winter, a bee starves to death before a honey shop.

- تموت جوعا نحلة في الشتاء أمام محل بيع العسل

131. Awareness is a sharp tool, usually hurtful.

الوعي أداة حادة كثيرا ما تجرح

132. Sometimes doors are open when you have no power left to enter.

أحيانا تفتح الأبواب حين لا نكون نقوى على الولوج

133. It's painful when a lumberjack tells a tree, he's about to cut down, that spring is near.

من المؤلم أن يبشر الحطاب الشجرة التي قطعها للتو بأن الربيع بات وشيكا

134. Try for once to wake up without opening your eyes, you'll see unimaginable things.

حاول مرة أن تستيقظ دون أن تفتح عينيك, سترى أشياء لم تتخيلها

135. Only the Bedouin is certain that he's here to leave.

وحده البدوي متأكد أنه جاء ليرحل

136. The mute runner dreams to reach the speed of sound.

- العداء الأبكم يحلم أن تصل سرعته لسرعة الصوت

137. Winter has reached its mid, and a polar bear is worn down by insomnia.

- انتصف الشتاء والدب القطبي مصاب بالأرق

138. He's been limping all his life, but has never fallen down.

- يعرج طوال عمره لكنه لم يسقط أرضا أبدا

139. I have grown to believe that only the aimless will arrive.

- بت أعتقد أنه لن يصل إلا الذي بلا وجهة

140. Whenever the runner ceased to run, he feels that he has lost his identity.

- كلما توقف العداء عن الجري شعر بفقدان الهوية

141. The blind kid believes that no one can see him when he ceases to move.

الطفل الكفيف يظن أن لا أحد يراه لمجرد توقفه عن الحركة

142. A blind man is amongst them, however none has noticed him.

بينهم الكفيف ولكن لم يلحظه أحد

143. A life boat remained tied to the sinking ship.

قارب النجاة ظل معلقا بالسفينة الغارقة

144. When a person starts hearing that he's actually looks younger, be sure that senescence is leaking unto him.

عندما يبدأ الإنسان بسماع: أنه يبدو أصغر سنا من الواقع, ثق أن الشيخوخة بدأت تتسرب إليه

145. A guy with cut off fingers cries bitterly over his string-less violin.

يبكي صاحب الأصابع المبتورة كمانه الذي أصبح بلا أوتار

146. Because of her overwhelming feeling of cheapness, the prostitute always attains grand auctions.

● لشعورها العارم برخصها, تواظب فتاة الليل على حضور المزادات الكبرى

147. How amazing wind is! It leaves its trace by erasing traces.

● ما أعجب الريح! تترك أثرها بأن تمحو الأثر

148. He has all wisdom, yet he does all the mistakes of the naïve.

● يجمع الحكمة ويرتكب أخطاء الساذجين

149. My old man was firm and strict in his words, but his hands, because of Parkinson, were always shaking.

● كان أبي العجوز حازما في كلامه, ولكن يديه, من فعل الباركنسون, ترتجف

150. An old worn-out shoe, the crippled wishes to wear it and go on.

● حذاء قديم ممزق يود المقعد لو ينتعله ويمضي

151.   Born and died in truce.

- ولد ومات في الهدنة

152.   The fruit that did not ripen nor fall nor harvested will face autumn's wind alone.

- الثمرة التي لم تنضج ولم تسقط ولم تقطف ستواجه رياح الخريف وحيدة

153.   It's clear that wind sweeps the traces of the passers... The strangers more.

- من الملاحظ أن الرياح تكنس آثار خطوات العابرين ...الغرباء أسرع

154.   The blind tells his friend that when he wants to stare at someone, he touches him.

- يخبر الكفيف أصدقاءه أنه حين يريد أن يحدق بشخص يلمسه

155.   After a hurricane, a gentle breeze tickles a hidden rose.

- بعد الإعصار نسمة تهز وردة مختبئة

156. Slow death in a rapid life.

موت بطيء في حياة سريعة •

157. The blind says: Life is a flash, a mere flash, and we cannot see it.

يقول الكفيف: الحياة وميض... مجرد وميض وليتنا نراه •

158. Open your eyes, you can see everything before you, close them and mull over the universe.

افتح عينيك يمكنك أن ترى كل الذي أمامك, أغمضهما وتأمل الكون •

159. A tree grows old, when deserted nests infest it.

تشيخ الشجرة عندما تكثر فيها الأعشاش المهجورة •

160. When his hand was cut off, he took it to the fortuneteller so she could read his fortune.

عندما قطعت يده حملها للعرافة لتقرأ له طالعه •

161. Despite all the twaddle we hear, humanity dies silently.

● رغم كل ما تسمع من ثرثرة, الإنسانية تموت بصمت

162. His culture is shallow, yet all his wounds are deep.

● ثقافته سطحية ولكن كل جراحه غائرة

163. Sad it is indeed, that we grasp high fruit only when they fall down.

● كم محزن أننا لا ننال الثمرة العالية إلا عندما تسقط

164. The sootiest darkness emits from quenched lanterns.

● الحلكة الأشد هي الآتية من المصابيح المطفأة

165. The disfigured looks at an accurate mosaic and weeps bitterly.

● مشوه ينظر إلى لوحة فسيفساء شديدة الدقة ويبكي

166. Rain was late, so a cactus bloomed.

تأخر المطر فأزهرت صبارة ●

167. Even the surrendered might really get his revenge.

حتى المستسلم قد يصدق وعيده بالانتقام ●

168. The sculptor has a stone-like lineaments.

النحات صاحب ملامح قاسية مثل الصخر ●

169. The painter is mean, whenever he sells a painting, he elegizes it with another.

الرسام لئيم كلما باع لوحة رثاها بلوحة اخرى ●

170. He always panics whenever he, the blind, remembers that when he dies, his eyes will remain open.

لطالما أفزع ذاك الكفيف أنه عندما يموت ستظل عيناه أبدا مفتوحتين ●

171. The deaf brags that he can approach the beehive and the buzzing won't disturb him, he forgot that bees sting too.

● يفاخر الأصم أنه يستطيع الاقتراب من خلية النحل كثيرا دون أن يزعجه طنينها, نسي أنها كذلك تلسع

172. Whenever a bee stings him, the beekeeper feels sorry that he didn't raise her well.

● كلما لسعته نحلة شعر مربي النحل بالحزن لأنه لم يحسن تربيتها

173. Whenever I get lost, I follow my trace to reach me.

● كلما تهت اتبعت آثار خطاي لأصل إلي

174. The painter with a back pain draws people, for revenge, carrying the burdens of life.

● الرسام الذي يؤلمه ظهره دوما, انتقاما يرسم الناس وهم يحملون أثقال الحياة

175. Who believes that a bee choose the hard way to reach a flower?

● من يصدق أن نحلة اختارت الطريق الأصعب للوصول إلى الزهرة

35

176. The boat that did not sink, brought back drowned people.

القارب الذي لم يغرق رجع محملا بالغرقى •

177. The passers only stopped to leave again.

لم يتوقف العابرون إلا لكي يواصلوا المسير •

178. The crippled dreams of walking even while sleeping.

المقعد يحلم أن يسير ولو نائما •

179. I never picked a single flower in my life, maybe because I want to steal honey.

لم أقطف زهرة في حياتي ربما لأنني أفكر أن أسرق شهد النحل •

180. Birds are the lashes of the sky.

العصافير رموش السماء •

181.   The window is an open eye, curtains shut it.

النافذة عين مفتوحة تأتي الستائر وتغمضها ●

182.   In autumn, a leaf sees off its fellows, for she'll be leaving with the next wind blow.

في الخريف ورقة شجر تودع رفيقاتها لأنها ستسافر بعيداً في هبة الرياح القادمة ●

183.   The old man stood before the calendar and tried hardly to remember where his life did go.

وقف العجوز أمام التقويم وحاول التذكر أين ذهب عمره ●

184.   The bee kept on buzzing in the deaf man's ear until he smiled.

ظلت النحلة تطن في أذن الاصم الى أن ابتسم ●

185.   Butterflies are flying paintings.

الفراشة لوحة تطير ●

186. Bashful she is and cannot look at him as they kiss, but she stares at their shadow on the wall.

تخجل أن تنظر إليه وهو يقبلها ولكنها تحدق بخيالهما على الجدار ●

187. All those flowers and bees in the painting and not a single droplet of honey.

كل تلك الزهور والنحلات في اللوحة ولا قطرة شهد ●

188. The questions of the mute's soul scream.

الأبكم أسئلة روحه تصرخ ●

189. The custodian of fire wishes for the butterflies to go away.

سادن النار يحلم أن يبتعد الفراش ●

190. The blind sees no dreams, but he interprets reality.

الكفيف لا يرى الأحلام ولكنه يؤول الواقع ●

191. Those who wage wars, be sure that they are dwelled with occupation.

- الذين يعلنون الحرب دوما ثق أنهم يسكنهم الاحتلال

192. The infertile woman is pondering fruitless trees.

- العاقر تتأمل الأشجار التي لا تثمر

193. The midwife's husband is an undertaker.

- الداية زوجها حانوتي

194. Many ends and not a single arrival.

- نهايات كثيرة ولا وصول واحد

195. For the river, arriving is not the prize; it's the explosion of the fount.

- بالنسبة للنهر الوصول ليس جائزة بل تفجر النبع

196. All his teeth have fallen, but he can't stop staring at a nut.

- سقطت كل أسنانه لكنه لا يستطيع أن يحرك ناظريه عن حبة بندق

197. A new world, a ratty home.

- عالم جديد ووطن بالٍ

198. It's time for weary boats to leave the dock and sink.

- آن للمراكب المتعبة في الميناء أن تغادر لكي تغرق

199. Near the one who died of thirst, a fount exploded and flowed until it quenched the cactus.

- بالقرب من الذي مات عطشاً تدفق النبع وسال حتى روى الصبار

200. Even the winner runner stumbled in a step.

- حتى العداء الفائز تعثر بخطوة

201. Even after the long applause, the maestro still thinks that there was a discord at a point.

- حتى بعد التصفيق الطويل ظل المايسترو يعتقد أنه كان هناك لحن خطأ

202. After the leprous was healed, he became afraid of handshakes.

- بعد أن شفي المجذوم أصبح يخشى مصافحة الناس

203. That student knows the answer, but he is not raising his hand, because his hand is cut off.

- يعرف ذاك الطالب الجواب ولكنه لا يرفع يده ليجيب, لا لشيء ولكن لأن يده مقطوعة

204. The deer is a part of the wolves gang, but he has no opinion regarding the hunting plan.

- الغزال فرد من قطيع الذئاب ولكنه لا يدلي برأيه في خطة الصيد

205. It's not a coincidence that the fount quenched the snake, it's because water dilutes poison.

- ليس صدفة أن يسقي النبع الأفعى, فالماء يخفف حدة السم

206. For some sort of wisdom, the fount in the depth of the ocean sacrifices itself to salt.

- لحكمة ما يهب نبع الماء في قعر المحيط نفسه للملح

207. The fount simply amazes me, how doesn't it fear that the thirsty will rush to devour it?

- كم يدهشني نبع الماء لعدم خوفه من تزاحم العطشى عليه

208. He wasn't moving fast, simply because he didn't want to exhaust the ones trailing him.

- لم يكن يحث الخطى كي لا يرهق من كان يتتبع خطواته

209. At least there are no civilian victims on the chess board.

- على الأقل ليس هناك قتلى مدنيين على رقعة الشطرنج

210. It's smart to notice that there is someone moving the King... on the chess board.

- من الذكاء ملاحظة أن أحداً يحرك الملك... في رقعة الشطرنج

211. For the wild bird the nest is a phase, the sky is home.

في عرف الطير البري العش مرحلة ....السماء وطن •

212. There are no shortcuts, but there are wasted steps.

ليس هناك درب مختصر ولكن هناك خطوات تذهب هباء •

213. The runner girl envies all dancers, because they can do a
step backwards.

العداءة تحسد الراقصات لأنهن يستطعن أن يقمن بخطوة للخلف •

214. A lonely night-guard wishing to meet a burglar.

حارس ليلي وحيد يتمنى لو يصادف لصا •

215. The beauty of the wild horse over the tamed one is that the
wild horse just runs, it does not want to arrive.

روعة الحصان البري عن حصان السباق أنه يجري ولا يريد أن يصل •

216. The loner practices yoga to get alone with himself.

الوحيد يمارس اليوغا لينفرد بذاته •

217. The loner bleeds time.

الوحيد ينزف الوقت •

218. The Hippy does not believe in pruning.

الهيبي لا يؤمن بفكرة تقليم الاشجار •

219. The mute old man has a crying baby in his soul.

العجوز الأبكم في روحه طفل يصرخ •

220. Why must the past always interfere with every decision of our future?

لماذا يجب على الماضي دوما أن يدلي بدلوه في كل قرار يخص المستقبل •

221.	A poor crippled man dreams of a mocking chair.

●	المقعد الفقير يحلم بكرسي هزاز

222.	I wasn't wasting my time, I was losing.

●	لم أهدر وقتي كنت أخسر

223.	The disfigured casts about in the faces of the crowd for anyone who looks like him.

●	المشوه يبحث بإصرار بين المارة عمن يشبهه

224.	Horrifying silence dominates there intense argument, my deaf & mute friends.

●	صمت مريع يسود نقاشهم الحاد, أصدقائي الصم البكم

225.	The mute complains to his mother that his scream has no echo.

●	يشكو الأبكم لأمه أن لا صدى لصراخه

226. He is acrophobic, died in a mine collapse.

عنده هلع الأماكن المرتفعة قتل بانهيار منجم عليه •

227. On the longest day of the year, the prisoner will be executed at dawn.

في أطول نهار في السنة سيعدم السجين ساعة الفجر •

228. The old dying crippled man weeps, because for the first time ever, he is going away.

يبكي العجوز المقعد المحتضر لأنه لأول مرة سيذهب بعيدا •

229. The old bold man is reading an article that hair keeps growing even after death.

العجوز الأصلع يقرأ مقالا إن الشعر يظل ينمو حتى بعد الموت •

230. In their times of happiness, strangers tend to silence.

دوما الغرباء بافراحهم يميلون للصمت •

231. The girl with paralyzed arms are only attracted to girls' nail polish.

مشلولة اليدين لا يشدها إلا ألوان طلاء أظافر الصبايا

232. He's colour blind, and he complains about it to his blind friend.

مصاب بعمى الألوان يشكو لصديقه الكفيف همه

233. He led a campaign against death penalty, but he committed suicide.

قاد حملة ضد عقوبة الإعدام ولكنه انتحر

234. Because the road is longer than you may imagine, it doesn't matter if you wore a shoe or not.

لأن الدرب أطول مما تتخيل, لا يهم إن انتعلت حذاءً أم لا

235. The loner might be the most aggressive.

قد يكون الوحيد الأشد عدوانية

236. A person may lose more than he can handle, and may gain more than he ever dreamt.

قد يخسر المرء أكثر مما يستطيع الاحتمال, وقد يربح أكثر مما يحلم به ●

237. The crippled just broke his leg.

المقعد كسرت رجله ●

238. An open lock, existential paradox.

قفل مفتوح تناقض الوجود ●

239. The custodian of fire has quenched eyes.

سادن النار مطفأ العينين ●

240. I do not believe the rumors about the one who committed suicide, that he was selfish.

لا أصدق ما يقال عن الذي انتحر, بأنه كان أنانياً ●

241. Amazing is this chess board, Clean! Without a single droplet of blood.

● مدهشة رقعة الشطرنج هذه, نظيفة بلا قطرة دم عليها

242. He stutters, but he's in a hurry.

● يتأتئ بالكلام ولكنه على عجلة من أمره

243. He only has four fingers, but decides to draw an octopus.

● بيده أربعة أصابع فقط ويرسم أخطبوط

244. The limp wishes he could walk, even for once, snootily.

● الأعرج يتمنى لو يمشي مرة بخيلاء

245. Nothing is as amazing as dawn; it gives you everything you need, a new start.

● لا شيء مذهل مثل الفجر يعطيك كل ما تحتاج... بداية جديدة

246. Darkness itself heralds dawn, but who can bear to wait?

العتمة ذاتها تبشر بالفجر , ولكن من يحتمل الانتظار؟ ●

247. Sometimes you have to quench your only candle so your soul will trust that dawn is nigh.

أحيانا يجب أن تطفئ الشمعة الوحيدة لديك لتثق روحك أن الفجر على ● الأبواب

248. How much does it take for the winning horse to realize that it lost the pride of the wild?

كم يلزم حتى يعلم الحصان الفائز بالسباق أنه خسر كبرياء البرية ●

249. Silk has hurt me, when I couldn't bestow it upon my lover.

جرحني الحرير عندما لم أستطع أن أهديه لحبيبتي ●

250. A blind peacock, nature's wisdom.

الطاووس الأعمى حكمة الطبيعة ●

251.   In steady pace we head towards stumble.

- بخطى ثابتة نذهب للتعثر

252.   Whenever the bachelor flips a card, he finds a queen glistening in all her temptation.

- الأعزب كلما قلب ورقة لعب خرجت له بنت بكامل زينتها

253.   Why doesn't the dam wit the thirst of all beings?

- لماذا لا يدرك السد عطش الكائنات؟

254.   A mute is reading passionately about language death.

- أبكم يقرأ بشغف بحثا عن موت اللغة

255.   The boat fastened to the deck moans more than the one fighting against drowning.

- يئن المركب المربوط في الميناء أكثر من ذلك الذي يصارع الغرق

256.   Since he was told he mutters in his sleep, the mute began going to bed early.

منذ أن قيل له إنه يتمتم في منامه أصبح الأبكم يذهب للنوم باكرا ●

257.   Even a giraffe does not see far enough.

حتى الزرافة لا ترى بعيدا بما يكفي ●

258.   The crippled is hanged from his legs.

المقعد معلق من قدميه ●

259.   In a world full of loses we become as butterflies, playing with fire.

في عالم مليء بالخسارات نصبح مثل الفراشات نلهو باللهب ●

260.   Nothing disturbs dreams more than reality.

لا شيء يشوش على الأحلام مثل الواقع ●

261. An atheist with all the holy books on his desk.

ملحد على مكتبه كل الكتب المقدسة •

262. The blind hates the pictures in which he appears closed-eyed.

يكره الكفيف الصور التي يبدو فيها مغمض العينين •

263. From the cemetery it was lunched, the protest against poor living.

من المقبرة انطلقت المظاهرة احتجاجا على سوء المعيشة •

264. Long distances' runner has his heart stopped in the onset of the race.

عداء المسافات الطويلة توقف قلبه أول السباق •

265. In the race of life, even the winner is late.

في سباق الحياة حتى الفائز متأخر •

266. A lone bird flying over a massive protest

- طائر وحيد يحلق فوق مظاهرة مليونية

267. He wants to suicide off the life boat.

- يود الانتحار من على قارب النجاة

268. Do not scorn humble boats, for they can get you to the other bank.

- لا تنظر إلى القوارب المتواضعة باحتقار فبإمكانها إيصالك إلى الضفة الأخرى

269. The opera singer is not convinced that he should stand a moment of silence to honor his murdered friend.

- المغني الاوبيرالي ليس مقتنعا بأنه يجب أن يقف دقيقة صمت حدادا على صديقه المقتول

270. The bird may not fly high but it can go far.

- قد لا يستطيع الطائر أن يحلق عاليا ولكنه يستطيع أن يبتعد

271. A ghost stood before a mirror and when he didn't see itself in it, he panicked as if he saw a ghost.

- وقف الشبح أمام المرآة وعندما لم ير نفسه فيها تملكه الفزع كمن يرى شبحا

272. Even the turtle is entitled to take a break.

- حتى السلحفاة من حقها أن تتوقف لتستريح

273. A step renders standing a history no matter how long it lasted.

- الخطوة هي التي تجعل الوقوف ماضيا مهما طال

274. Even our pets do not feel grateful, for they offer us a favor as well.

- حتى حيواناتنا الأليفة لا تشعر أنها مدينة لنا بشيء فهي أيضا تقدم لنا خدمة

275. The mute woman wears plenty of perfume... so it may speak out.

- تضع البكماء كمية عطر كبيرة... ليبوح

276.	Even the lost has acolytes.

- حتى التائه له أتباع

277.	Even the crippled awaits the coming step.

- حتى المقعد ينتظر الخطوة القادمة

278.	The miserable clown will keep torturing the crowd with laughter until they cry.

- المهرج البائس سيظل يعذب المتفرجين بالضحك حتى يبكوا

279.	Even on the brink we hide a wish that we – maybe unconsciously- want to step ahead.

- حتى على حافة الجرف نخفي أمنية أننا نود – ربما دون وعي – أن نتقدم خطوة

280.	Wild horses' tamer, completely tamed by life.

- مروض الخيول البرية روضته الحياة تماما

281. My shadow has never departed my side, but has never shaken my hand.

   - ظلي لا يفارقني ولكنه لم يصافحني يوما

282. The lone wolf is the most ferocious in attacking groups.

   - الذئب الوحيد الذئب الأشرس في مهاجمة الجموع

283. It's terrifying to see a look of defeat in the eyes of the blind.

   - من المرعب رؤية نظرة انكسار في عيني الكفيف

284. The loner is trying to resurrect some souls.

   - الوحيد يحاول استحضار بعض الارواح

285. Beneath the chess board, a mass cemetery.

   - أسفل رقعة الشطرنج مقبرة جماعية

286. Even when we're lost, there is still a path we walk.

• حتى عندما نتوه, ثمة درب ما نسلكه

287. Trees do not compete only in growing tall, but also in hanging to the ground.

• لا تتسابق الأشجار بأن تعلو في الفضاء فقط, ولكنها تتسابق أيضا بأن تتشبث بالأرض

288. A supernumerary is leading a protest in a film.

• كومبرس في فيلم يقود المظاهرة

289. A shadow is not sure; in the real world is he real or mere fantasy?

• لا يعرف الظل هل هو في عالم الواقع حقيقة أم خيال

290. Even a caterpillar can't explain silk.

• حتى دودة القز لا تعرف أن تشرح الحرير

291. Bleeding won't last, no matter what, it won't last.

• لن يستمر النزف... بأي حال لن يستمر

292. The loner is standing before a mirror and taking a picture of two.

• الوحيد يقف أمام المرآة ويلتقط صورة لشخصين

293. The soldier who lost his arm in the battle has found his comrade's head while searching for his arm.

• الجندي الذي فقد قدمه في الحرب وجد رأس زميله في بحثه عنها بعد الانفجار

294. Everybody wants a parrot that can talk. Except the mute, he wants a parrot that listens well.

• الكل يريد ببغاءً تتكلم إلا الأبكم يريد ببغاءً تحسن الإصغاء

295. A bird left the herd, not for a disharmony in the looks, nor in the horizon.

• طائر ترك السرب ليس لنشاز في المنظر وليس لنشاز في الأفق

296. A cacophony broke the silence.

- لحن نشاز كسر الصمت

297. A cacophony in the orchestra, maybe a solo presenting
another musical aspect.

- لحن نشاز في الاوركوسترا, ربما يكون منفردا يمثل وجهة نظر موسيقية
أخرى

298. Endings taught me not to be fond of arriving.

- علمتني النهايات ألا أكون مغرما بالوصول

299. Nothing acquires the full attention of the blind more than a
quenched candle.

- لا شيء يلفت انتباه الكفيف إلا الشمعة المطفأة

300. Sometimes the real thing that a traveler needs to arrive is
not water, its thirst.

- أحيانا لا ينقص المهاجر كي يصل قربة ماء, ولكن العطش

301. Two obstacles in a single step.

عثرتان في خطوة واحدة •

302. Since ages the road is standing before the house, yet it never dared to knock the door.

منذ أمد يقف الطريق أمام البيت ولا يجرؤ أن يطرق الباب •

303. From far, boats disappear and people seem to be having their own battles with the ocean.

من بعيد تختفي القوارب ويبدو البشر وكأنهم يخوضون معركتهم مع المحيط •

304. The one-eyed cannot take chances in accepting the idea of an eye for an eye.

لا يستطيع الأعور أن يجازف بقبول فكرة العين بالعين •

305. On my way to lying, I passed by truth.

في طريقي للكذب مررت بالحقيقة •

306. He almost died by thirst thus the flood tempted him.

● كاد يقتله العطش لذا فتنه الطوفان

307. The crippled is dreaming of a miracle so he can walk... On water!

● المقعد يحلم لو أن المعجزة تحصل معه ويسير... على الماء

308. The disfigured became a runner, so he may become a passing man with no features in the eyes of the passers.

● المشوّه أصبح عداءً كي يبدو للمارة بلا ملامح...مجرد رجل يعدو

309. The runner is afraid of getting lost amid standers.

● العداء يخاف أن يتوه بين الواقفين

310. The bat does not herald darkness, but different visions.

● لا يبشر الخفاش بالعتمة ولكن برؤى مختلفة

311. The little boy with a toothache forgets the pain completely when he sees an elephant's tusk.

الطفل الذي يؤلمه سنه ينسى ذلك تماما عندما يرى ناب الفيل ●

312. The more I walk through this road the more I feel that the ones who made it were going back.

كلما سرت إلى الامام بالدرب زاد شعوري بأن من اختطوا هذا الدرب كانوا ●
راجعين

313. In the very beginning, someone whispered in the ear of silence.

في البدء همس أحد في أذن الصمت ●

314. Even the snow man is entitled to dream of a warm day.

حتى رجل الثلج يحق له أن يحلم بنهار دافئ ●

315. From the entire herd, one swallow alit on the string of a kite to rethink about his destination.

سنونو واحد من بين السرب توقف على خيط الطائرة الورقية المحلقة ليعيد ●
التفكير بوجهته مرة أخرى

316. It's not a masquerade, but these are certainly not human faces.

- ليست حفلة تنكرية ولكنها ليست بالتأكيد وجوه بشر

317. The more I realize that talking is useless, the more I blabber.

- كلما تأكدت أكثر أنه لا فائدة من الكلام صرت ثرثارا

318. In this short age, I have not seen but congestion of seasons.

- في هذا العمر القصير لم أر سوى ازدحام الفصول

319. Away from all blabber, a rose blooms mutely.

- بعيدا عن الثرثرة تتفتح زهرة بصمت

320. A broken branch needs more than a splint; it needs a bird to sing on it.

- الغصن المكسور يحتاج لأكثر من جبيرة, يحتاج لعصفور يغرد عليه

321. While he swings his ax towards the tree, the lumberjack is not sure if he is with or against euthanasia.

- وهو يهوي بفأسه على الشجرة لا يعرف الحطاب بالضبط هل هو مع القتل الرحيم أم ضده

322. To battle, entire nations march unto defeat.

- إلى المعركة تذهب أمم بأكملها للهزيمة

323. The lefty lumberjack cuts down all trees on his right.

- الحطاب الأعسر يقطع كل الشجر الذي على يمينه

324. You don't need a dictionary to find the synonym of crying.

- لا تحتاج لقاموس لتعثر على مفردة "البكاء"

325. The lost did not find anything, not even mirage.

- التائه لم يجد حتى السراب

326. A long dead end.

- طريق طويل مسدود

327. The mute, while in a protest, loves to be filmed while holding the speaker.

- يعشق الأبكم وهو بالمظاهرة أن يتم تصويره وهو ممسك بمكبر الصوت

328. By loss we are freed from the illusions of perfection.

- بالخسارة نتحرر من أوهام الكمال

329. The moment when the boat sank was the exact moment in which it thought it found land.

- اللحظة التي غرق فيها المركب ذاتها اللحظة التي ظن انه استدل فيها على اليابسة

330. I never saw a more expressive look than the look of the deceased unto life.

- لم أر نظرة معبرة أكثر من نظرة الميت للوجود

331.   The most assertive moments in life are the ones in which we did not make a decision.

● اللحظات الأكثر حزما في الحياة هي تلك التي لم نتخذ فيها أي قرار

332.   How much I wish to go away, far away, where I can approach everything.

● كم أتمنى الذهاب بعيدا بعيدا حيث يمكن الاقتراب من كل شيء

333.   Some silence teaches rhetoric.

● بعض الصمت يعلمك بلاغة اللغة

334.   I am late only when someone is waiting for me.

● لا أتأخر إلا حينما يكون هناك من ينتظرني

335.   He survived the flood, but is ashamed to say that he's thirsty.

● الناجي من الفيضان يخجل أن يبوح أنه عطش

336. From the aperture of his cell, the prisoner looks at the empty crossroad and cries.

• من كوة سجنه ينظر السجين لمفترق الطرق الخاوي ويبكي

337. Without the caprice of youth I head to the poise of old age.

• بلا نزوة الشباب اذهب لوقار الشيخوخة

338. A crippled kid sitting on the floor and throwing his brothers' shoes from the window.

• طفل مقعد يجلس على الأرض ويرمي أحذية إخوته من النافذة

339. He suffers from chronic insomnia, but he interprets dreams well.

• مصاب بأرق مزمن ولكنه يفسر الأحلام جيدا

340. The one-eyed man is amazed by the broadness of the scenes in dreams.

• مندهش هو الأعور من حجم اتساع المشاهد في الحلم

341.   Who can say: coincidence is late?

من يستطيع أن يقول: لقد تأخرت الصدفة! •

342.   A tunnel starting and ending in the same besieged city.

نفق يبدأ وينتهي داخل نفس المدينة المحاصرة •

343.   Only he, among all of the murdered's family, kept visiting the grave for long years... The hitman.

وحده القاتل من بين كل الناس- حتى ذوي القتيل- ظل يزور القبر سنوات • طوالا

344.   I am lost, but I feel the ecstasy of the explorer.

لقد ضللت الطريق ولكني أشعر بنشوة المستكشف •

345.   The hitman says: when my bullet misses, it hits me.

يقول القاتل المأجور: عندما تخطئ طلقتي سوف تصيبني •

346. The most devious fox is the one still "wearing" its fur.

الثعلب الأمكر هو الذي ما زال "يلبس" فراءه •

347. Even the paths we did not step on may determine the fate of our steps.

حتى الدروب التي لم نطأها ربما تحدد مصير خطانا •

348. Bees look at honey shops as dins of thieves.

ينظر النحل لمحلات بيع العسل كوكر للصوص •

349. A bird can handle being homeless but not wingless.

يحتمل العصفور أن يكون بلا عش ولكن ليس بلا جناح •

350. Forties are good times not only to slow down, but to change direction as well.

الأربعينيات وقت مناسب ليس فقط لتخفيف الاندفاع ولكن أيضا لتغيير الاتجاه •

351. The one-eyed man said: with one eye you can see everything, even the hidden.

يقول الأعور: بعين واحدة يمكنك أن ترى حتى المختبئ •

352. Even ghosts have their own mirrors that show them and do not show humans.

حتى الأشباح لهم مراياهم التي تظهرهم ولا تظهر البشر •

353. A ghost that believes in the cloche of invisibility.

شبح يؤمن بطاقية الاخفاء •

354. After long drought and after rain has pelted down, a thirsty seed is chocking.

بعد الجفاف الطويل وبعد أن يهطل المطر بذرة عطشى تختنق •

355. In this life even if you gave up, the battle will go on.

في هذه الحياة حتى وإن استسلمت ستستمر المعركة •

356. He owns a lot, he who thinks he deserve freedom.

- يملك الكثير الذي يعتقد أنه يستحق الحرية

357. The son of the drowned is surrounding the sea by paintings of lifeboats on the beach.

- ابن الغريق يحاصر البحر برسومات قوارب النجاة على الشاطىء

358. At the bird park and when I see an eagle in a cage unfolding its lofty wings, only black comedy crosses my mind.

- في حديقة الطيور وعندما أشاهد نسرا في القفص يفرد جناحيه الطويلين, لا يخطر في بالي إلا فكرة الكوميديا السوداء

359. Withstanding life makes history, at least your history.

- صمودك أمام الحياة يصنع التاريخ, على الأقل تاريخك

360. In the journey of thirst even empty wells are tempting.

- في رحلة العطش حتى الآبار الفارغة لها كلمة مسموعة

361. No matter how high the kite flew, it knows that it's tied.

مهما حلقت الطائرة الورقية, هي لا تنسى أنها مربوطة ●

362. Lighten your burden of dreams, so you can carry them.

تخفف من الأحلام كي تستطيع حملها ●

363. In some sorts of standing, some sort of arrival.

في بعض الوقوف شيء من الوصول ●

364. The bleeding wolf is the one that will avenge the entire pack.

الذئب النازف الذئب الذي سيأخذ بثأر الزمرة كلها ●

365. Do not hasten hunting; there is a green branch that will, One day, be your arrow.

لا تستعجل الصيد فهناك غصن ما زال أخضر, سيصير ذات يوم سهمك ●

366. There is anger in the eyes of that sleeping blind man.

ثمة غضب في عيني ذاك الكفيف النائم •

367. The arrow is never hesitating, even if it missed.

السهم لا يكون مترددا وإن طاش •

368. The hunter panics before the deer that dies peacefully.

مذعور هو الصياد أمام الغزال الذي يحتضر بطمأنينة •

369. The deer does not understand the concept 'amateur hunter'.

لا يفهم الغزال معنى جملة صياد هاو •

370. There is a bee that had to sting and die before producing a single droplet of honey.

هناك نحلة قبل أن تنتج نقطة عسل اضطرت أن تلسع وتموت •

371. Even great loses require great spirits.

حتى الخسارات العظيمة تحتاج أرواحا عظيمة

372. He that has gone astray left an inerasable track.

الذي تاه ترك أثرا لا يمحى

373. The old butterfly alit on the wilting rose.

الفراشة العجوز تقف على الزهرة الذابلة

374. Even in negligence there is a plea.

حتى في الغفلة رجاء

375. The thief raises a dog that barks at police men.

اللص يربي كلبا ينبح كلما مر رجل شرطة

376. The flowing river is part of the tranquility.

النهر في جريانه جزء من السكون

377. Bleeding will eventually stop, true wounds are scars.

سيتوقف النزف في لحظة ما, الجروح الحقيقية هي الندوب

378. Before he leads a protest, he ponders alone.

قبل أن يقود المظاهرة يختلي بنفسه

379. The scar-less in this life was simply hiding from them.

الذي بلا ندوب في هذه الحياة كان يختبئ منها

380. He mutters but his eyes glitter in firmness.

يتأتئ ولكن ترى في عينيه الحزم

381. Do not be a rash! Even the road took some time to arrive.

• لا تستعجل حتى الدرب أخذ وقته ليصل

382. He is secretly a part of an anti-violence society... the soldier.

• ينتمي سرا لجمعية تناهض العنف... هو العسكري

383. We heal slowly from the wounds we never cried from.

• إننا نشفى ببطء من جراحنا التي لم نبكِ من أجلها

384. In battle, the solider that attempted suicide was executed.

• في المعركة تم إعدام الجندي الذي حاول الانتحار

385. He entered the battle as a vegan, but he killed many people.

• دخل المعركة نباتيا ولكنه قتل الكثيرين

386. We are in constant war against ourselves; even sleep might not be a truce.

إننا نخوض معركة دائمة مع ذواتنا حتى النوم قد لا يكون هدنة ●

387. Sometimes I have to lie at myself, because I am afraid to face myself.

اضطر أحيانا لمداهنة ذاتي خوفا من مواجهتها ●

388. The most terrifying thing for a walker is a crossroad.

أكثر ما يخيف السائر مفترق الطرق ●

389. A loner suffers from abundance of dreams.

وحيد يشكو كثرة الأحلام ●

390. Do not expect the rose to bloom just because you watered it.

لا تنتظر من الوردة أن تتفتح بمجرد أنك رويتها ●

391.   What does the buzzing want me to hear?

- ماذا يريد الطنين منك أن تسمع؟

392.   In the labyrinth, the marching of the runner means nothing.

- في المتاهة لا يعني شيئاً تقدم العداء

393.   Arriving many times is a sign of digression.

- كثرة الوصول دليل تيه

394.   I wonder! Do we lose the butterflies that escaped the net?

- ترى أنخسر الفراشات التي هربت من الشبكة

395.   A single seed denies absolute death.

- بذرة واحدة تنفي الموت المطلق

396. The mute is overjoyed because his newborn son just screamed.

- الأبكم سعيد جدا أن وليده لحظة ولادته يصرخ

397. Some people and as soon as they hear the word 'Marathon' they begin to gasp.

- هناك من الناس ما إن يسمع كلمة سباق المراثون حتى يبدأ باللهاث

398. There is digression after arrival.

- هناك تيه ما بعد الوصول

399. Even our death won't last long, how about life?

- حتى موتنا لن يطول فما بالك بالحياة

400. The burned lady stands before the mirror in pitch darkness and weeps bitterly.

- المحترقة تقف أمام المرآة بالعتمة وتجهش بالبكاء

401. The leaf sacrificed itself to fall off the tree to become, just for a moment, a butterfly.

جازفت الورقة بنفسها لكي تسقط من الشجرة لتصبح ولو لبرهة فراشة

402. Don't be sad, some of the birds in cages do not want to fly.

لا تحزن كثيرا فبعض الطيور التي في الأقفاص لا تريد أن تحلق

403. When the sun shines over the cemetery, everybody has overslept.

عندما يطلع الصباح على المقبرة الكل متأخر بالنوم

404. When Fortresses expire, they crack.

عندما تنتهي مدة القلاع تبدأ بالتصدع

405. I do not feel lost, but walking is useless.

لا أشعر بالتيه ولكن بلا جدوى المسير

406. At the zoo, a leopard looks scornfully at a runner.

في حديقة الحيوان ينظر الفهد للعداء نظرة استهزاء ●

407. A hungry man brooding at a picture of a mouldy apple.

جائع يتأمل لوحة تفاحة فاسدة ●

408. The son of the lumberjack is plucking many flowers.

ابن الحطاب يقطف كثيرا من الزهور ●

409. The toter smiles because his boss didn't notice the limp in his leg.

يبتسم الحمال رغم الأثقال التي يحملها لأن رب عمله لم ينتبه أنه أعرج ●

410. The noblest thing to do with a flag is to shroud a citizen.

إن أنبل ما يمكن عمله بالعلم ستر عري مواطن ●

411. He is a blubber because he has nothing to say.

- ثرثار لأنه لا يجد ما يقول

412. In the paths of life, the obstacles we could not overcome will always be before us.

- في دروب الحياة العثرات التي لم نستطع تخطيها دائما ستكون أمامنا

413. The foundling is a genealogist.

- اللقيط نسابة

414. How could've believed it! The loner is a telltale.

- من يصدق... الوحيد نمام؟

415. The blind is the only one among his brothers who wakes up at dawn.

- الكفيف وحده من بين إخوته الذي يستيقظ على الفجر فجأة

416. The rose tells me: Do not be sad, I would've wilted even if you did not pluck me.

تقول الوردة لي: لا تحزن كنت سأذبل حتى لو لم تقطفني ●

417. Sometimes, despair is our savior.

أحيانا قد ينجينا اليأس ●

418. Since the dawn of time, we are fighting by the fount, and we're all still thirsty.

منذ فجر التاريخ ونحن نقتتل عند نبع الماء وما زال الكل عطشى ●

419. Maybe because there are no borders in the horizons, pigeons fly between the church and the mosque.

ربما لأن لا حواجز في الأفق تطير أسراب الحمام بين المسجد والكنيسة ●

420. Founts – although important – they do not determine the destination of caravans.

الينابيع – على أهميتها – لا تحدد وجهة القوافل في الصحراء ●

421. Whenever a bee stings me, I crave honey more.

●   كلما لسعتني نحلة صرت شرها أكثر لأكل العسل

422. How sadistic the inventor of the vase is!

●   ساديّ هو من اخترع المزهرية

423. There is sadness in the touch of silk.

●   ثمة حزن في ملمس الحرير

424. My guard dog barks a lot, maybe because it sees many thieves.

●   ينبح كلب الحراسة لدي كثيراً, ربما لأنه يرى كثيراً من اللصوص

425. As a punishment for the guard dog, the thief stands at length in front of it.

●   كعقاب لكلب الحراسة المربوط يقف أمامه اللص طويلا

426. Because you have a guard dog, does that mean you're not a thief?

هل مجرد اقتنائك كلب حراسة ينفي عنك فكرة أنك لص ●

427. The deeper the river, the smoother and quieter it flows.

كلما كان النهر أكثر عمقا انساب بهدوء وسكينة ●

428. The fount is the river's grandfather.

النبع جد النهر ●

429. The river marches sluggishly, maybe it wants to go back.

ينساب النهر بتثاقل, ربما لأنه يريد أن يعود ●

430. When a river realizes there is no going back, it flows like a waterfall.

عندما يدرك النهر أن لا سبيل إلى الرجوع يندفع كشلال ●

431. The fire is quenched and not a single butterfly flew around it.

انطفأت النار ولم تحم حولها مرة فراشة ●

432. The butterfly led the kids to fire, they quenched it and the butterfly went on.

الفراشة دلت الصبية على النار لتطفئها ومضت ●

433. With a low voice he waged war.

بصوت منخفض يعلن الحرب ●

434. He did not accept armistice, and he announces surrender.

لم يقبل الهدنة... ويعلن الاستسلام ●

435. Even open doors must be knocked.

حتى الأبواب المفتوحة يجب أن تُطرق ●

436. The sun does not declare surrender, it just sets.

- الشمس لا تعلن الاستسلام, تغيب فقط

437. Some humans are much like stagnant water; a mere shack is enough to release the odor of decay.

- بعض البشر مثل البحيرة الراكدة, أي تحريك له ينشر رائحة العفن

438. Don't stare at the light, but at what it has lit.

- لا تحدق في النور, ولكن فيما أنار

439. How would a quenched lantern rescue its sanity out from a pitchy night?

- كيف يخرج قنديل مطفأ عاقلا من ليلة مظلمة؟

440. Some butterflies hover around darkness.

- بعض الفراش يحوم حول العتمة

441. Even lifeboats are not well-made.

● حتى قوارب النجاة ليست متقنة الصنع

442. The tree's crookedness may protect it against the lumberjack.

● قد يحمي الشجرة من الحطاب اعوجاجها

443. The storm that quenched all lanterns is the same that carried the spark unto the woods.

● العاصفة التي أطفأت القناديل ، نفسها التي حملت شرارة للغابة

444. Coldness is part of the rituals of darkness.

● البرد جزء من طقوس العتمة

445. Are you sure that your candles are enough against darkness?

● أمتأكد أن شموعك تكفي لتبدد العتمة؟

446. The Snowman has no childhood.

- رجل الثلج بلا طفولة

447. Some lashes make you adore closed eyes.

- بعض الرموش يجعلك تعشق العيون المغلقة

448. Even a broken thorn enkindles sadness.

- حتى الشوكة المكسورة تبعث على الأسى

449. The captain's ship has sunk while he was reading about the one who walked on water.

- الربان غرقت سفينته وهو يقرأعمن مشى على الماء

450. The clown makes people laugh, so crying can come more painful.

- المهرج يضحك الناس ليأتي البكاء أكثر وجعا

451.   You won't take anything with you out of this life, so do not be afraid of losing.

   ● لن تأخذ شيئا معك بعد الحياة فلا تجزع من الخسارة فيها

452.   How knows? Maybe chance missed me?

   ● من يدري ربما أخطأتني الصدفة!

453.   Even amid ruins, you may find the base brick.

   ● حتى بين الأنقاض قد تجد لبنة الأساس

454.   That you're amid ruins, does not mean you are about to fall.

   ● لا يعني أنك بين الخراب أنك آيل للسقوط

455.   I do not want to arrive, if I'll wait there a lot.

   ● لا أريد الوصول... إن كنت سأنتظر هناك طويلا

456. If you were patient while you walk, do not think you won't be patient while you arrive.

- اذا كنت تتأنى في المسير, لا تعتقد أنك لن تتأنى في الوصول

457. Even when you lose, you are entitled to rest.

- حتى عندما تخسر من حقك أن تستريح

458. Do not venture into others' paths, even if you did not arrive.

- لا تسر في درب غيرك وإن لم تصل

459. Hope does not enlighten darkness; it merely makes you search for the lantern.

- الأمل لا ينير العتمة ولكنه يجعلك تبحث عن القنديل

mohannad.alazab@hotmail.com

https://twitter.com/mohannadalazab1

https://www.facebook.com/mohannad.alazab